P9-DFL-971

THE
WEATHER
GIRLS

TO SEBASTIAN, MY DREAM CATCHER . . .

THE WEATHER GIRLS

Aki

Henry Holt and Company

New York

Laura

Miffy

Annie

Rebecca

Jane

Vanessa

June

Melanie

MEET THE WEATHER GIRLS

Sarah

Cathleen

Lucy

Zoe

Kirsten

Tilly

Joy

Emily

It's summertime. We rise and shine!

All set to go, we form a line.

A big, bright sun.

Let's have some fun!

We swim and dive and splash and run.

Lush green forest, fresh clean air.
Look at all the creatures there!

Fall is windy in the city.
Trees are gold and red and pretty.

It's time for sweaters and for fun.

Through fallen leaves
we run and run!

We hop on bikes and ride and ride.

We pick apples

side by side.

Wintertime brings lots of snow.

Brrrr, brrrr, girls.

Let's go, go, go!

Through a blizzard, climb and climb.

The mountain's tall.

It takes some time.

The snow has stopped,
and we do, too.

The sky is big and bright and blue.

Spring is springing
through the trees.

We can feel the gentle breeze.

A big balloon!

Hooray,

hooray!

Up we go; we float away.

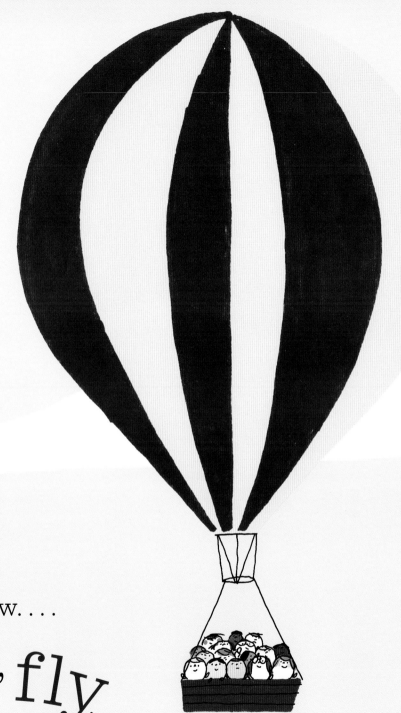

Strong winds blow....
We fly, fly, fly.

Now look up—

a rainbow sky.

MEET THE SEASONS

WINTER, SPRING, SUMMER, FALL—THE WEATHER GIRLS LOVE THEM ALL!

SUMMER

We see lots of animals out and about.

Plants are greenest. Temperatures are highest.

Days are longest. Sunshine is strongest.

FALL

We see fewer animals. Leaves change colors
and fall from the trees. Temperatures are cooler.
Days get shorter. There's less sunshine.

WINTER

Many animals hibernate or travel for warmer weather. Some trees and plants are bare of leaves. Temperatures are coldest. Days are shortest. Sunshine is weakest.

SPRING

We start to see more animals. Trees and plants grow new leaves and become greener. Flowers bloom. Temperatures are rising. Days get longer. There's more sunshine.

Henry Holt and Company

Publishers since 1866

Henry Holt® is a registered trademark of Macmillan Publishing Group, LLC

175 Fifth Avenue, New York, New York 10010

mackids.com

Copyright © 2018 by Aki

All rights reserved.

Library of Congress Cataloging-in-Publication Data is available.

ISBN 978-1-62779-620-0

Our books may be purchased in bulk for promotional, educational, or business use.
Please contact your local bookseller or the Macmillan Corporate and Premium
Sales Department at (800) 221-7945 ext. 5442 or by e-mail at MacmillanSpecialMarkets@macmillan.com.

First edition, 2018 / Designed by April Ward
Printed in China by RR Donnelley Asia Printing Solutions Ltd., Dongguan City, Guangdong Province

1 3 5 7 9 10 8 6 4 2